Garglejuice

Paul Stewart is the very funny, very talented author of more than twenty books for children, including *The Edge Chronicles*, a collaboration with Chris Riddell.

Chris Riddell is a well-known illustrator and political cartoonist. His work appears in the *Observer* and the *New Statesman*, and he has illustrated many picture books and novels for young readers.

Both live in Brighton, where they created the Blobheads together.

Titles in the Blobheads series

All Blobheads titles can be ordered at your local bookshop or are available by post from Book Service by Post (tel: 01624 675137).

^{The} Blobheads

Garglejuice

Paul Stewart
and Chris Riddell

MACMILLAN
CHILDREN'S BOOKS

P.S. For Joseph and Anna
C.R. For Katy

First published 2000 by Macmillan Children's Books
a division of Macmillan Publishers Limited
25 Eccleston Place, London SW1W 9NF
Basingstoke and Oxford
www.macmillan.co.uk

Associated companies throughout the world

ISBN 0 330 38976 9

1 3 5 7 9 8 6 4 2

A CIP catalogue record for this book is available from
the British Library.

Typeset by SX Composing DTP, Rayleigh, Essex
Printed and bound in Great Britain by Mackays of Chatham plc, Kent

Chapter One

"You know your trouble," said Derek, shaking his blobby head gravely. "You don't get out enough."

Kevin the hamster tutted with irritation. "Of course I don't. That's because *I'm always locked inside this blooming cage*," he said loudly for Billy's benefit.

Billy put down his comic. "It's for your own good," he sighed. "You know what happened last time. That could have been a very nasty accident."

"*Hmmph!*" Kevin huffed. "Maybe I *wanted* to see the inside of the vacuum cleaner."

"Whatever," said Billy. "Don't let him out again, Derek." He frowned. "And put my baby brother down."

"Can't," said Derek. "I'm a dummy."

"You can say that again," snorted Kevin the hamster.

"No, I mean, I'm a *dummy*," said Derek. "Look! The High Emperor just loves chewing on my tentacle."

Sure enough, there was Silas chewing gummily on the Blobhead's tentacle, making soft cooing noises. Billy groaned. "As if my life isn't complicated enough already," he muttered.

It wasn't easy sharing a bedroom with three red and purple aliens who had arrived from the planet Blob,

convinced that Silas, Billy's baby
brother, was the High Emperor of the
universe – and matters had taken a
definite turn for the worse when
Derek taught his pet hamster to talk!
Now, to crown it all, Silas was teething.

What with Silas's screaming and
Kevin's constant chatter, Billy had
been kept awake most of the previous
night. And the night before that . . .

Just then, Kerek and Zerek burst into the room carrying a toothbrush and a tube of toothpaste.

"Is it here yet?" Kerek asked excitedly. "Has it arrived?"

"What?" said Billy.

"The High Emperor's first tooth, of course," said Kerek.

"Not yet," said Derek. He inspected his bruised tentacle. "But it won't be long now."

"Waaaah!" Silas screamed. He grabbed the tentacle, stuffed it back into his mouth and began chewing all the harder.

The three Blobheads beamed at him proudly.

"In that case, it won't be long before the High Emperor is invited to the dentist," said Kerek.

"That won't be for ages," said Billy.

"Though *I'm* going tomorrow."

The Blobheads turned on him in surprise.

"You have an invitation?" said Kerek. "*You?*"

"We didn't think you were important enough," said Zerek.

"Of course I am," said Billy. "Everyone's important enough to go to the dentist."

Clearly shocked by this latest piece of information, the three Blobheads huddled together, the blobs on their huge heads pulsing with red and purple light.

"What's the matter?" said Billy.

Kerek turned to face him. "The Great Computer clearly states that only the most important people are invited to dentists' parties."

"Parties?" said Billy.

"Come on, Billy," said Zerek. "We know all about dentists' parties. The fun. The games." He sighed dreamily. "And best of all, of course, the garglejuice!"

"Mmmm, garglejuice," the three Blobheads murmured, and licked their beaky lips.

"I don't know about that," said Billy. "*I* go to the dentist to make sure my

teeth are clean and healthy. He looks inside my mouth with a little mirror on a stick. Prods about a bit—"

"Yes, yes," said Zerek impatiently. "That's not important. You get garglejuice there, don't you? The Great Computer is quite clear on the matter . . ."

Billy frowned. It wasn't the first time that the Blobheads' so-called *Great* Computer had been wrong. "What is this garglejuice?" he said.

"What is *garglejuice?*" Zerek spluttered, unable to believe his listening-blobs. "It's only the most delicious drink in the known universe."

"Yum!" slurped Derek, his mouth watering.

"Garglejuice is so rare, so precious, it is only found on Earth at the place you call the dentist," said Kerek. "Scrumptiously refreshing, it is. A purple, perfumed mouthwash that—"

"Mouthwash?" said Billy surprised. "You mean the stuff you get when the dentist's finished looking at your teeth. The stuff you swill round your mouth and spit out."

The Blobheads started back in disbelief. Their blobs fizzed and buzzed.

"You spit it out!" said Kerek. "The nectar of the galaxy, and you spit it out! What an appalling waste!"

"Absolute madness!" Zerek agreed.

"I'd give my right tentacle if I could try garglejuice just once," said Derek, his mouth watering even more.

"Stop dribbling on my brother's head," said Billy.

"Sorry," said Derek. "Oh, but

garglejuice. *Gaaaargle*juice!" He slurped noisily. "Billy, will you take me to the dentist with you?"

"Typical," said Zerek. "Always thinking of yourself."

"Will you take *all* of us?" asked Kerek.

"No," said Billy.

"We promise to be good," said Zerek. "Don't we?"

The three Blobheads nodded enthusiastically.

"No," said Billy.

"Please," said Derek.

"No!" said Billy.

"Pleeeease!" they all said together.

"Pretty please," added Kevin the hamster.

"NO!"

Chapter Two

The following afternoon, when he heard his dad beeping the horn outside, Billy grabbed the red and purple blobby hat, scarf and jacket and rushed downstairs. He didn't notice that the door to the hamster cage was ajar or that, for once, Kevin was silent.

As always, the Blobheads had morphed into everyday objects that they hoped would blend in. As always, they had got it wrong. It was a sunny day, yet Billy was dressed for the Arctic. When he climbed into the car, his dad looked at him curiously.

"What on earth are you wearing that lot for?" he said. "You must be sweltering."

Billy shrugged. "They wouldn't take no for an answer," he muttered.

Mr Barnes shook his head. "I've said

it before and I'll say it again: you are a strange boy, Billy Barnes."

Billy smiled. Better that his dad thought he was a bit weird than discover the truth about the Blobheads. "It's not that hot," he said.

"Not that hot?" said Mr Barnes. "It's *baking* . . . Speaking of which, I've got a treacle and Gorgonzola upside-down cake in the oven. If the traffic's bad in town, I'll drop you off at the corner. All right?"

"All right, Dad," said Billy.

"Mum'll pick you up at five."

Billy nodded.

The traffic *was* bad in town that afternoon and Billy had to complete his journey on foot. With Kerek disguised as the scarf, Zerek as the jacket and Derek a bobble hat, Billy was dripping with sweat by the time he reached the dentist's.

"Couldn't you have morphed into something a bit cooler?" said Billy crossly as he pushed the dentist's door open. He pulled the bobble hat from his head.

"How about this, then?" said Derek. Billy found himself holding a fluffy blue toy kangaroo. "Pretty cool, eh?"

Billy sighed. "Trust you!" he said. He shoved it under his arm. "Now, don't wriggle," he instructed. "And keep quiet."

"Quiet as a louse," said Derek.

"*Mouse*," Billy corrected him.

"Where?" said the scarf.

"Nowhere," said Billy.

"But—"

"As quiet as a mouse," he said. "That's what people say."

"But a mouse isn't quiet," said the jacket. "It squeaks . . ."

"Whereas a louse is always as silent as the gravy," said the fluffy blue toy kangaroo.

"Will you *all* be quiet!" Billy hissed. "If you can't be good, then I'm taking you back home right now!"

The three Blobheads fell silent. So close to tasting garglejuice for the very first time, they weren't about to mess up now.

"Thank you," Billy whispered. "Now stay quiet."

He walked into the reception area and looked around. There were five people waiting there. A teenager with a broken front tooth. A red-haired girl with her red-haired father. A bony old man who was making strange sucking noises. And a short portly woman with

a swollen jaw, who sat in the corner, moaning softly to herself.

Billy crossed the room to the reception desk.

"And you are?" said the receptionist, looking up.

"Billy Barnes."

The receptionist checked her lists. "Ah, good," she said. "One for Mr Wilberforce. If you were here to see Mrs Malone, you'd have a long wait."

At that moment, there was a loud *buzz* and the blue light on her desk flashed.

"Excellent," she said. "You can go straight up. Surgery 1."

The dental nurse – a young woman with flyaway hair and pink cheeks – greeted him at the door.

"Billy?" she said. Billy nodded.

"Come in, then."

Billy went inside.

"Afternoon," said Mr Wilberforce.

"Afternoon," said Billy.

"Now then," said the dental nurse. "We'll take off that scarf and jacket, shall we?"

Billy slipped them off, handed them over and glared at them severely as they were hung over the back of the chair by the door. For everyone's sake, he hoped that Kerek and Zerek would behave.

"And . . . errm. . ." the dental nurse continued, "shall I take the . . . erm . . . kangaroo, is it?"

"Yes, it is a kangaroo," said Billy. "And no, I'll keep hold of it, thanks."

"Come on now," she said, her cheeks getting pinker. "A big boy like you!"

She wrenched the fluffy blue toy kangaroo away. Derek squeaked uncomfortably.

"We'll put him over here on the table, so you'll still be able to see him."

"No!" said Billy insistently. "It really would be *much* better if I kept hold of him." He snatched him back. "Believe me!"

Mr Wilberforce nodded to his assistant that it was all right; he could hold onto his fluffy toy if he wanted.

"Nervous, are we?" he said.

"*I'm* not," said the kangaroo. "Just thirsty—"

Billy clamped his hand firmly round the kangaroo's nose. "Well, maybe a little nervous," he said.

Mr Wilberforce chuckled affably. "Well, there's nothing to be worried about." He nodded to his dental

nurse. "It's Miss Parfitt's first day here – she's probably more nervous than you! Jump up onto the chair. That's it. Now, open wide . . ."

Billy did as he was told. As Mr Wilberforce prodded about, the fluffy blue toy kangaroo noticed a movement out of the corner of his eye. It was the jacket and the scarf. They were sliding down off the back of the chair, slithering across to the door, slipping outside . . .

"Hey, you two," he cried out. "Wait for me!"

At least, that was what he *tried* to cry out. At the first sound he made, however, Billy squeezed his muzzle tightly shut. "*Unnh-unnh!*" Derek mumbled.

The dentist withdrew his mirror and prodder. "Sorry?" he said.

"Nothing," said Billy. "Just my tummy rumbling." He smiled. "I just wish it would KEEP QUIET!" he said. Derek squirmed about. "And STAY STILL!"

Mr Wilberforce glanced at his dental nurse and raised one eyebrow. Derek stopped moving.

"That's better," said Billy. He opened his mouth wide again.

The dentist continued with the check-up. The fluffy blue toy kangaroo remained absolutely still.

So far, so good, Billy thought.

Derek was transfixed. There, just out of reach, on a stand beside the reclining chair, was a glass of purple liquid. It was garglejuice!

And it was his, all his!

Outside on the landing, the scarf and jacket morphed back into Kerek and Zerek.

"That was boring!" said Kerek, shaking his blobby head.

"And not a drop of garglejuice to be seen," said Zerek. "Fine dentist *he* is!" He pointed to the door marked Surgery 2. "Let's try in there."

Slowly, cautiously, they crept across the landing. Below them, a buzzer sounded. Kerek reached up, pressed the handle and pushed the door. He peeked into the empty room.

"All clear," he whispered. "And look! *There's* the garglejuice." He nodded towards a large bottle of purple liquid on a shelf. "I—"

"Is that you, Mrs Gimble?" came a voice from the cupboard in the far corner of the room.

"That must be Mrs Malone," Kerek whispered. "The other dentist."

"I'll be right with you," she was saying. "I'm just trying to find your file."

The Blobheads went into the room. The dentist was standing in the doorway of the cupboard, her back turned.

"And you must excuse me for running so late this afternoon," she went on, as six little feet puttered across the tiles towards her. "My dental nurse fell ill earlier and I'm trying to carry on single-handed."

Six purple tentacle-arms rose up into the air.

"Do take a seat," she said.

Six purple tentacle-arms took her by the arms.

"What the . . . ?" Mrs Malone gasped.

Six purple tentacle-arms guided her gently, but firmly, into the cupboard. Zerek closed the door. Kerek turned the key in the lock.

"Alone at last!" he exclaimed. "Time for that garglejuice . . ."

There was a knock on the surgery door. Kerek and Zerek looked at each other.

"Who is it?" Kerek asked.

"It's Mrs Gimble," came the reply. "The receptionist told me to come up."

Zerek turned to Kerek. "What do we do now?"

Chapter Three

"Excellent," said Mr Wilberforce. His dental nurse made a note on the chart of Billy's teeth. "Absolutely nothing to worry about here."

Billy clamped his hands round the kangaroo snout tighter than ever. The dentist smiled.

"Relax, young man," he said. "Your teeth are fine. You've been taking excellent care of them. Now we'll just see how your molars are doing and then you can rinse out with some mouthwash."

Derek quivered in Billy's arms.

"Steady!" the dentist chuckled. "Soon be finished." He removed the mirror and prodder from Billy's mouth and turned to the dental nurse for a closer look at the chart.

The moment his back was turned Derek seized his chance. He reached out a fluffy blue paw towards the glass of purple mouthwash, and grasped it. Just then a small furry face appeared from his pouch.

"*Pfwoooah*!" Kevin exclaimed. "This pouch is worse than my cage!"

Miss Parfitt glanced round. "*Waaaaah*!" she screamed. Derek dropped the glass of mouthwash. It smashed on the tiled floor.

"A mouse!" shrieked Miss Parfitt.

"Miss Parfitt!" exclaimed the dentist.

"Kevin!" shouted Billy.

"Garglejuice!" wailed the blue kangaroo.

"Are you ready for me, then?" said Mrs Gimble from the landing outside Surgery 2.

"No . . . I mean, I don't know . . . I mean, yes," came a voice. It sounded flustered, and was followed by a lot of muffled bumping and clattering. "You'd better come in."

Mrs Gimble opened the door. She looked round uncertainly. There before her were two somewhat blobby figures in white coats. One of them was holding out a tray of drinks.

"Garglejuice?" he said.

Mrs Gimble didn't move. "You're not Mrs Malone," she said.

"No," the figure without the tray agreed. "But . . . we're dentists," he said eagerly. "I'm Mr Kerek. And this is Mr Zerek, my assistant. We were just having some garglejuice, if you'd care to join us."

"Why am *I* always *your* assistant?" said Zerek. "Why can't *you* be *my* assistant for once?"

"Be quiet, Zerek, and just pour the garglejuice!" said Kerek impatiently.

Zerek did as he was told, filling three glasses with the purple liquid. Kerek took one. Zerek took another.

"No thank you," said Mrs Gimble as Mr Zerek offered her the third.

"As you please," he said.

The two blobby dentists clinked their glasses together, cried "Blobs up!" and took a long, long slurp.

"Wow!" gasped Kerek.

"Deeeeee-licious," purred Zerek. "Go on," he said, shoving the tray under Mrs Gimble's nose. "Have some!"

"No, really, Mr Zerek, I—" Mrs Gimble began. From the cupboard, there came a low groaning noise.

"What was that?" she said.

"What was *what?*" said Kerek and Zerek together. They each took a second slurp of the garglejuice.

The noise came again, muffled and unclear – followed by a soft tapping sound.

"That!" said Mrs Gimble.

"Oh, *that*," said Kerek. "That's . . . *hic* . . . That's . . . Now, what are they called? Little furry things, scuttle around in corners, like cheese . . . *hic* . . ."

"Hamsters!" said Zerek.

"Hamsters?" said Mrs Gimble suspiciously.

"But never mind about them," said Kerek cheerily. He drained his glass, poured himself another and waved the bottle at Mrs Gimble. "Are you sure I can't tempt you?"

Mrs Gimble shook her head. "I don't want anything to drink," she said. "I just want you to do something about this terrible toothache."

"Oh, all right," said Kerek disappointedly. "Climb onto the chair, then."

Mrs Gimble sat down in the big dentist's chair. The tapping from the inside of the cupboard grew louder.

Kerek smiled. "Noisy little creatures, hamsters, aren't they? They're up half the night. They never stop talking." He had a slurp of garglejuice. "I sucked one up in a vacuum cleaner recently . . ."

But Mrs Gimble wasn't listening. "Aren't you going to recline the seat?" she said.

"Recline the seat?" said Kerek. "You mean, put the back of the seat down? Ah, yes, here we are."

He pressed a lever and hoped for the best. The seat abruptly tipped backwards. Mrs Gimble cried out and clutched at her throbbing tooth.

"Whoops!" said Kerek. "Bit *too* far." He pressed the lever a second time.

With a jolt, the backrest sprang upwards, catapulting Mrs Gimble forwards and launching her off the chair.

"Ooooh!" she squeaked as she tumbled forwards, and – THUD! – landed on the floor.

"*Waaaah!*" said Zerek, falling back against the wall in surprise. His blobby head bumped the buzzer-button.

Downstairs, the receptionist looked up. She saw the flashing red light on her desk.

"That was quick," she said to herself. "Still . . ." She looked down her list. "Mr Lewis," she said.

The bony old man looked up.

"If you'd like to go up, Mrs Malone will see you now."

Back in the surgery, Zerek was beside himself. "Blobby Heavens!" he exclaimed and hurried towards her. "Are you all right?"

Mrs Gimble moaned, her eyelids fluttered and she looked up dazed. "Is that you, Ethel?" she muttered.

"That's the spirit," said Kerek. "Now drink your garglejuice."

Across the landing in Surgery 1, Mr Wilberforce – down on all fours – was far from happy.

"You're a very silly boy, Billy," he said. "A fluffy toy's one thing, but bringing your pet is quite another." He turned to his dental nurse. "Miss Parfitt, please try to pull yourself together."

"A mouse!" sobbed Miss Parfitt, balancing unsteadily on top of her stool. "It could be anywhere! Find it!" she shrieked. "*Find it*!"

"That's exactly what we're trying to do," said Mr Wilberforce, as he reached underneath the reclining chair.

Billy was on his hands and knees over by the desk. "He's a hamster," he said, "not a mouse. Kevin. Kev-in!"

From the chair, the fluffy blue toy kangaroo looked down miserably at the broken glass and spilt garglejuice.

"It's all *her* fault," he muttered.

"Derek!" said Billy.

"Derek?" said Mr Wilberforce. "Did you say 'Derek'? I thought his name was Kevin. Just how many rodents *have* you brought with you?"

A ball of golden fur darted along

the skirting board between the table and the sink.

"There it is!" shouted Mr Wilberforce, lunging forwards. Billy skidded across the floor to head him off.

The fluffy blue toy kangaroo leant over and tapped Miss Parfitt on the leg. "I don't suppose there's any more garglejuice going?"

"*Waaaah!*" Miss Parfitt screamed as she tottered precariously on the stool. "Something soft and furry touched my leg and . . . Oh, help!" she cried, crashing to the floor.

Mr Wilberforce leapt to his feet. "Miss Parfitt!" he said. "Miss Parfitt, are you all right?"

Chapter Four

"It spoke to me," Miss Parfitt sobbed, her eyes darting anxiously all round the room. "It tapped me on the leg – and then spoke to me."

"There, there," said Mr Wilberforce, patting her hand awkwardly.

"It *did*," she said, sitting up. "I heard it. It wants . . . garglejuice."

"Of course it does," said Mr Wilberforce soothingly.

Billy seized the fluffy blue toy kangaroo by the paw and peered round the room. The longer Kevin the hamster remained missing, the more convinced Billy became that he was up to something.

"You're just a little overwrought," Mr Wilberforce said as he helped the flustered dental nurse to her feet.

"But I did feel something," Miss Parfitt said.

"I'm sure you did," said Mr Wilberforce.

"Oh, and look!" said Miss Parfitt, bursting into tears. "The patients' notes are all over the floor."

"Never mind," said Mr Wilberforce.

"But I so wanted everything to run smoothly," she sobbed. "Today of all days."

The dentist chuckled. "I remember *my* first day," he said. "I was so nervous,

I could barely drill straight."

Miss Parfitt smiled bravely.

"Come on, now," said Mr Wilberforce. "I'll give you a hand."

Mr Wilberforce collected up the pieces of paper and, still shaking, Miss Parfitt attempted to get them into some sort of order.

On the other side of the room, Kevin the hamster finally found what he was looking for.

"*Psssst*, Derek!" he hissed.

Billy and the fluffy blue toy kangaroo looked up. Kevin was up on the shelf by the open window, leaning nonchalantly against a five-litre container of purple mouthwash with one paw, the plastic screw-on top in the other.

"Yes!" Derek exclaimed. He wriggled out of Billy's grasp and bounced

towards the shelf. "Garglejuice, here I come!"

Mr Lewis walked into Surgery 2.

"It's my dentures," he said. "They're just not right. They don't fit properly."

He stopped. His mouth fell open.

Two blobby dentists and the woman he'd noticed earlier in the waiting room were clustered together by the cupboard in the corner. The dentists seemed to be helping the woman to her feet, totally unaware that he had entered the room.

"What do you mean you don't want any garglejuice?" one of them was saying. "How can you resist?"

"I just don't," the woman snapped.

"Very peculiar, Mr Zerek," he said. "She doesn't seem to like garglejuice."

"All the more for us then, Mr Kerek," replied the other. "It's *so* delicious." He looked up and saw Mr Lewis. "Oops . . . *hic*," he said. "Here's another one."

Mr Lewis frowned. "What's going on?" he said. A muffled hammering came from the cupboard. "And what's that noise?"

Zerek sighed with exasperation. "Oh, not you as well. We've already explained that. *Hic*. Hamsters."

"And I'm telling you, you mean *mice* not *hamsters*," said Mrs Gimble.

"You're wrong," said Kerek. "Mice squeak. Hamsters speak. *Hic*. It's a well-known fact."

"Anyway, it doesn't sound like mice to me at all," Mrs Gimble persisted. "It sounds like someone's locked inside!"

"The very idea!" Zerek groaned as he struggled to pick Mrs Gimble up from the floor. "*Hic*. I . . . *unnkh*!" he grunted as he stumbled against the wall. His blobby head bumped the buzzer-button.

Down in the waiting room, the receptionist frowned. "Most peculiar," she said. She looked up at the teenager with the broken front tooth. "Vincent James," she said. "Mrs Malone will see you now."

"Oh, no," he groaned.

Back upstairs, Kerek turned to Mr Lewis and stumbled forwards. He raised the half-full bottle of purple liquid. "Garglejuice," he announced loudly. "Nectar of the universe—"

"Let me out!" came a muffled voice from the cupboard.

Mr Lewis backed away, open-mouthed, and groped for the door. At that moment there was a knock. The door opened and Vincent James blundered in, head down, hands in pockets – and, *boof*, walked straight into Mr Lewis.

The sudden jolt sent his ill-fitting false teeth leaping from his open mouth. They soared across the room.

"Well I never!" exclaimed Kerek.

"*Waaaaah*! He's falling to bits!" shouted Zerek, staggering back. His

blobby head bumped the buzzer-button for the third time.

"Good grief," the receptionist muttered to herself. "Mrs Malone's certainly getting through them today! Mr Blevins," she said. "If you'd like to take Belinda up now."

Billy had Derek by the tail. "Come here!" he shouted.

At the same moment, Mr Wilberforce spotted Kevin the hamster on the shelf.

"You won't get away this time!" he roared.

Miss Parfitt dropped her bundle of papers and scrambled back onto the stool. Mr Wilberforce lunged, made a grab for the hamster – and tripped over Billy.

CRASH!

The container of mouthwash wobbled from side to side, before toppling over by the open window. Derek watched in horror as the rare and precious, scrumptiously refreshing, purple, perfumed garglejuice gushed out of the five-litre container and down onto the street below.

"NO!" he wailed.

*

"I'm really sorry," said Vincent James. "I never look where I'm going."

"By benpures," Mr Lewis wailed gummily, as he crawled around the floor. "Pind by benpures!"

The hammering on the cupboard door grew louder, and the voice more insistent than ever. "LET ME OUT OF HERE!"

"I *knew* there was someone in there," said Mrs Gimble, tugging at the cupboard door.

"Honestly!" said Mr Zerek, reclining lazily in the dentist's chair. He took another large slurp of garglejuice. "It's nothing. Just hampers," he slurred. "I mean, *hamsters*. Tha'sall . . ."

The door to the surgery opened again and Mr Blevins came in, with Belinda trailing reluctantly behind him.

"They just keep on coming," Kerek laughed jovially, and staggered towards them. "Garglejuice all round?" he said.

At that moment, behind them, the lock gave way and the cupboard door flew open. Mrs Malone stumbled out, red-faced and dishevelled. She bumped into Mr Blevins and Belinda.

"What on earth is going on?" she yelled.

"We've only just got here," said Mr Blevins. "Haven't we, Belinda?"

Belinda burst into tears.

"So have I," agreed Vincent James.

"It was those *other* dentists," Mrs Gimble insisted.

"*What* other dentists?" Mrs Malone demanded.

"The blobby ones," said Mrs Gimble. "Mr Kerek and Mr Zerek—"

"WHO?" bellowed Mrs Malone.

They all looked around. There was a red and purple blobby scarf lying across the dentist's chair; a red and purple blobby jacket over the door. But of the two dentists, not a trace.

From the corner of the room came a plaintive voice. It was Mr Lewis. "Who trod on my benpures?" he said.

Chapter Five

No one in Surgery 1 noticed the door opening, nor saw the scarf and jacket slipping quietly through the narrow gap.

Billy was standing over by the dentist's chair, with Kevin the hamster in one hand and Derek the fluffy blue toy kangaroo in the other. He was ready to go.

"Don't forget your jacket and scarf," said Mr Wilberforce. "Oh, dear," he said. "They must have slipped off the chair." He brushed them down and hung them over Billy's arm.

"Thanks," said Billy. At least *two* of the Blobheads had been behaving themselves.

"Now remember, hamsters belong in cages not dentist surgeries," Mr Wilberforce was saying. "Still, cute little fellow . . ." His voice trailed off as he noticed his dental nurse pulling off her green dental coat. "Miss Parfitt?" he said.

"I resign!" she announced.

"I'll be off, then," said Billy, slipping out of the door before Mr Wilberforce decided to blame him for losing his new assistant.

"*Hic.*"

Pausing only briefly to listen to the clamour of voices coming from Surgery 2, Billy made his way to the

top of the stairs. There, he slipped his
jacket on, stuffed Derek and Kevin in
the pockets and hung the scarf
around his neck.

"*Hic.*"

Billy frowned and looked round. "Is
that you, Kerek?"

"No – *hic* – it's me, Zerek," said the
jacket. From the scarf came the sound

of soft snoring. Zerek giggled. "Kerek's asleep. It must have been all the excitement," he yawned.

"Hmmph!" said Billy, as he set off down the stairs. If the Blobheads had been bored, they only had themselves to blame. He'd told them not to come.

The waiting room was all but empty. Mrs Barnes looked up from the bench opposite.

"Hello, Mum," said Billy. "The dentist says my teeth are fine and . . ." He paused. "Mum?"

"Yes, Billy?"

"You're soaking wet!"

"I know I'm soaking wet," she said crossly. "Just as I was walking in through the door I got drenched! Some clot was pouring mouthwash out of an upstairs window!"

Billy frowned guiltily. "Someone's

idea of a joke," he said.

"Yes, well," said Mrs Barnes, throwing a furious glance at the receptionist. "I don't think it's funny. Come on, Billy, let's go home."

No one spoke on the journey back. Mrs Barnes was wondering how she would ever get the purple stain out of her suit. Billy was wondering whether the school jumble sale would accept a hamster and a toy kangaroo. And Kevin the hamster was wondering whether he'd ever be allowed out of his cage again.

The only noise to be heard was the soft, slurpy sound of a fluffy blue toy kangaroo sucking on the hem of a soggy jacket.

It wasn't until bedtime, when the Blobheads had morphed back and the hamster was in his cage once more, that Billy had a chance to tell Derek and Kevin exactly what he thought of their behaviour.

"I mean, why couldn't you have been like Kerek and Zerek?" he said. "*They* were good."

"No they weren't," said Derek. "I saw them—"

"Derek!" said Zerek sharply. "Don't

make matters worse by telling lies."

"But I did see them!" said Derek, waving his tentacles about agitatedly.

"*Waaaah!*" screamed Silas indignantly, as the comforting tentacle abruptly disappeared from his mouth.

Derek plugged it back in.

"Anyway," said Billy. "That's the last time I take you lot to the dentist's."

"Spoilsport," Kevin the hamster muttered sulkily from his cage.

"And as for *you!*" said Billy. "You're grounded! Another word out of you and you'll be the prize exhibit on the white elephant stall at the school jumble sale."

"My lips are sealed," said Kevin innocently. "And now, if you'll excuse me, I've got a thrilling appointment with a hamster wheel." He sighed. "Will the excitement never end?"

from the gum.

"Now we'll *have* to go back to the dentist's again!" said Zerek.

"Oh, no you won't!" said Billy. "And this time, when I say 'no', I mean 'no'. Absolutely not. No, no, no! Not in a month of Sundays. Never, ever . . ."

But the Blobheads weren't listening. Blobby heads pulsing with red and purple light, they opened their mouths and uttered one single word together.

"*Garglejuice*!"

At that moment, Derek let out a yelp and yanked his tentacle from Silas's mouth.

"That hurt!" he said.

"Wonderful news!" said Kerek. "The High Emperor's first tooth has arrived."

Silas looked up and grinned. One small, shiny white tooth was poking up